Hold Tight, Bear!

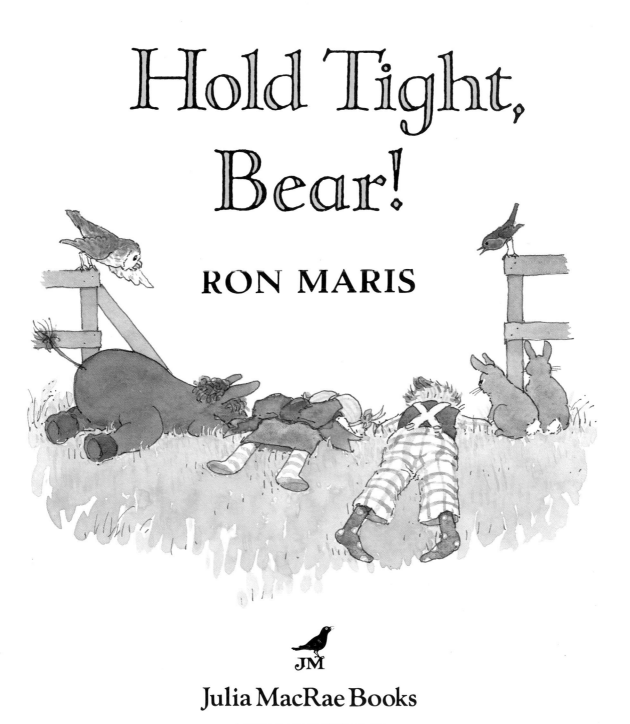

RON MARIS

JM

Julia MacRae Books

A DIVISION OF WALKER BOOKS

For some very nice people indeed

Copyright © 1988 Ron Maris
All rights reserved
First published in Great Britain 1988
by Julia MacRae Books
A division of Walker Books Ltd
87 Vauxhall Walk, London SE11 5HJ
Reprinted 1989

British Library Cataloguing in Publication Data
Maris, Ron
    Hold tight, bear!
    I. Title
    823'.914[J]
ISBN 0-86203-362-4
Printed and bound in Italy by L.E.G.O., Vicenza

Bear and Raggety,

Little Doll and Donkey,

are going for a picnic.

Over the fields,

across the stream,

to a meadow near the woods.

Donkey is drowsy.

Raggety is tired.

"Where are you going, Bear?"

Bear walks under the tall trees,

through the cool quiet woods.

"Is anybody there?"

"Watch where you're going, Bear."

"Look out! You'll fall..."

Over and over, and BUMP!!!

...but I can't climb up there."

"There they are, still fast asleep."

"Wake up, lazy Donkey!"

"How did you get down there, Bear?"

"We must pull Bear up," says Raggety.

"We can't reach down," says Owl.

"I know how!" says Little Doll.

"Wrap my sash round Donkey."

"Hang your bottom over there."

"Now reach down with your tail."

"Hold tight, Bear!" shouts everyone.

"Now everybody, PULL!"

"Thank you all," says Bear.

"Home for tea," says Raggety.

"Shall I tell you again how very brave I was?" said Bear.